The Sleepover Party

LITTLE TIGER PRESS

London

Little Monkey was having a
sleepover party and Little
Tiger, Little Elephant and
Little Leopard were invited.

Little Elephant couldn't wait. "Is it bedtime?" he asked for the fifth time.

At last it really was bedtime, and Little Monkey and Mummy Monkey showed them how to climb up to their beds.

Little Tiger and Little Leopard
scrambled up the tree but . . .

Little Elephant was left at the bottom!
"Help!" he trumpeted. "I can't climb trees!"
"Don't worry, Little Elephant," they all said,
sliding down the tree. "We'll help you."

The three friends pushed Little Elephant's bottom, and Mummy Monkey pulled his trunk. Little Elephant had almost reached the first branch when . . .

he slipped and fell to the ground.
"It's no good, I can't do it," cried
Little Elephant sadly.

But Little Tiger
had another idea . . .

Little Tiger collected some strong leaves while Little Monkey and Little Leopard found some vines.

They all helped Mummy
Monkey make a . . .

sling!
"Ready?" asked Little Tiger.
Little Elephant looked doubtful.
"One . . . two . . . three . . . PULL!"

They all pulled, and slowly
Little Elephant rose into the
air. He had almost reached
the second branch when . . .

SNAP!
The vine broke and Little
Elephant fell to the ground.
"Ouch!" he cried. "That
didn't work either."

"Never mind," said Little Leopard
brightly. "I've got a brilliant idea!"

Little Leopard found
a piece of wood and
balanced it on a stone.

Little Elephant sat on one end
and everyone else jumped on
the other end. Little Elephant
flew into the air and . . .

THUMP!

He crashed
back down to
the ground.
He sat there,
feeling dazed.

"I don't think I want to sleep in the trees," he said in a very small voice. "I think I'd rather stay here."

Little Monkey, Little Tiger,
and Little Leopard looked down
from their beds high in the trees.
"Poor Little Elephant," said Little
Monkey. "He looks very lonely."

"Hey! I've got a wonderful
idea!" cried Little Tiger . . .

So Mummy Monkey helped the
friends move their beds down
to where Little Elephant was.

"What fun!" said Little Tiger happily. "Now
we're having a sleepover and a camp as well!"
But Little Elephant was already fast asleep.

Written by Julie Sykes
Illustrated by Czes Pachela, based on the
characters created by Tim Warnes

LITTLE TIGER PRESS
An imprint of Magi Publications
1 The Coda Centre, 189 Munster Road, London SW6 6AW
www.littletigerpress.com
First published in Great Britain 2001
Text © 2001 Julie Sykes
Illustrations © 2001 Magi Publications
All rights reserved • Printed in Singapore • ISBN 1 85430 761 4
1 3 5 7 9 10 8 6 4 2